Florence FRIZZBALL

CLAIRE FREEDMAN

JANE MASSEY

Florence FRIZZBALL

For Lara, my lovely editor x - **CF**

For Lucy Hall - **JM**

SIMON & SCHUSTER

First published in Great Britain in 2017 by Simon and Schuster UK Ltd, 1st Floor, 222 Gray's Inn Road, London, WC1X 8HB • A CBS Company • Text copyright © 2017 Claire Freedman • Illustrations copyright © 2017 Jane Massey • The right of Claire Freedman and Jane Massey to be identified as the author and illustrator of this work has been asserted by them in accordance with the Copyright, Designs and Patents Act, 1988 • All rights reserved, including the right of reproduction in whole or in part in any form • A CIP catalogue record for this book is available from the British Library upon request • 978-1-4711-4453-0 (HB) • 978-1-4711-4454-7 (PB) 978-1-4711-4455-4 (eBook) • Printed in China • 10 9 8 7 6 5 4 3 2 1

Florence FRIZZBALL

Claire Freedman & Jane Massey

SIMON & SCHUSTER

London   New York   Sydney   Toronto   New Delhi

Hello! My name is Florence,

I have **frizzy, fuzz-ball** hair.

It's wild.

It's thick.

It's crazy.

And it sticks out everywhere.

My little brother's not like me,

Ben's hair is neat and flat.

We like to eat such different foods,

is it because of that?

When I pull my jumper on Ben laughs,

"It's so dramatic!"

My hair's electrifying

as it **crackles** with the static!

It's fun to race down grassy slopes
and feel the fresh wind blowing.

But it's not fair – with frizzy hair . . .

. . . I can't see where I'm going!

We love our **cosy** cuddle times,
but hugs turn **very** tickly.
My nightmare hair flies everywhere –

our faces get all **prickly!**

I searched through family photographs
for curls and frizzy fluff,

but no one else has hair like mine –
except for our dog, Scruff!

No matter what, my hair's a pain.

Ben moans it's in his way!
"Your frizzball always blocks my view

and I can't see!" he'll say!

I'm fed up of my curly hair. "Oh Mum, please let's go here.

A hairdresser might know a way to make frizz disappear."

They smooth

and spray

and struggle.

And . . .

voila!

Is this MY hair?

But Ben's SO shocked to see me
that he dives behind the chair.

And now it's neat, like all my friends . . .

Oh dear, I'm thinking twice.
I liked to stand out from the crowd –

it made me feel quite nice.

Straight hair has its problems too,

and mine gave Ben **a scare.**

But worst, he says I've lost my bounce . . .

I miss my frizzy hair.

Now I've got the kind of hair
I wanted for so long,

I thought that I'd be happier,
how could I be so wrong?

But as the rain pours down, Ben shrieks,

"Your hair is back – hooray!

I love you, Frizzball, as you are!"

"And so do I!" I say.